By the Light of the
Halloween Moon

by Caroline Stutson
illustrated by Kevin Hawkes

Amazon Children's Publishing

Text copyright © 2012 by Caroline Stutson
Illustrations copyright © 2012 by Kevin Hawkes
First Amazon Children's Publishing paperback edition, 2012

First published in 1993 by Lothrop, Lee, & Shepard Books

Amazon Publishing
Attn: Amazon Children's Publishing
P.O. Box 400818
Las Vegas, NV 89149
www.amazon.com/amazonchildrenspublishing

Library of Congress Cataloging-in-Publication Data
Stutson, Caroline.
  By the light of the Halloween moon / by Caroline Stutson ; illustrated by Kevin Hawkes. — 1st ed.
     p. cm.
  Summary: In this cumulative tale, a host of Halloween spooks, including a cat, a witch, and a
ghoul, are drawn to the tapping of a little girl's toe.
978-0-7614-5553-0 (hardcover) 978-0-7614-6244-6 (paperback)
  [1. Halloween—Fiction. 2. Stories in rhyme.] I. Hawkes, Kevin, ill. II. Title.
  PZ8.3.S925By 2009
  [E]—dc22
                         2008022965

Book design by Vera Soki

Printed in Malaysia (T)
10 9 8 7 6 5 4 3 2 1

For Al and Alec! — C.S.
For Susan Pearson — K.H.

A toe!
A lean and gleaming toe
That taps a tune in the dead of night
By the light, by the light,
By the silvery light of the Halloween moon!

A cat!
A thin black wisp of a spying cat
Who eyes the toe
That taps a tune in the dead of night
By the light, by the light,

A witch!
A watchful witch with streaming hair
Who snatches the cat
When he springs through the air to catch the toe
That taps a tune in the dead of night
By the light, by the light,
By the silvery light of the Halloween moon!

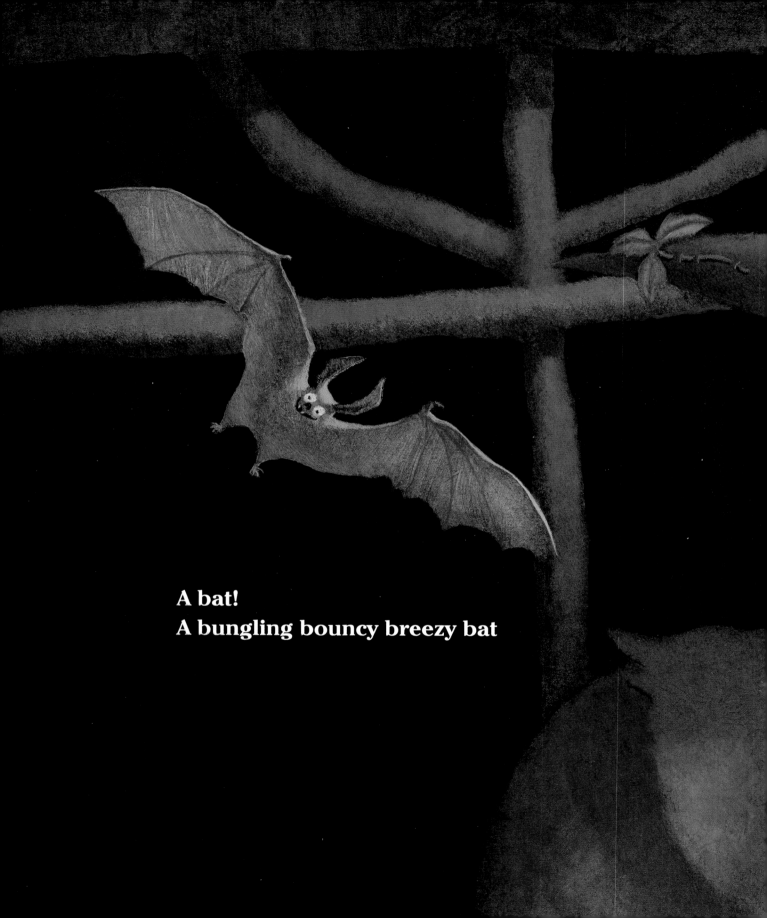

A bat!
A bungling bouncy breezy bat

Who bumps the witch as she snatches the cat
When he springs through the air to catch the toe
That taps a tune in the dead of night
By the light, by the light,
By the silvery light of the Halloween moon!

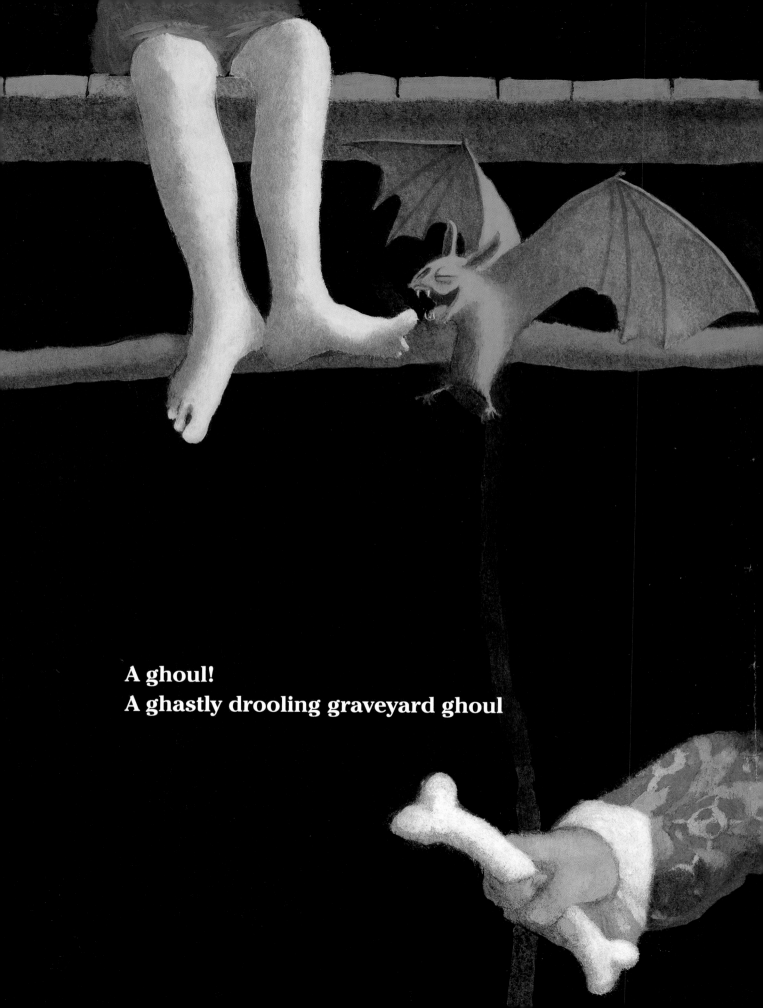

A ghoul!
A ghastly drooling graveyard ghoul

Who swats at the bat
Who bumps the witch as she snatches the cat
When he springs through the air to catch the toe
That taps a tune in the dead of night
By the light, by the light,
By the silvery light of the Halloween moon!

A ghost!
A williwaw ghost

Who trips the ghoul
Who swats at the bat
Who bumps the witch as she snatches the cat
When he springs through the air to catch the toe
That taps a tune in the dead of night
By the light, by the light,
By the silvery light of the Halloween moon!

A sprite!
A grumpy grungy hobgoblin sprite

Who bites the ghost
Who trips the ghoul
Who swats at the bat
Who bumps the witch as she snatches the cat
When he springs through the air to catch the toe
That taps a tune in the dead of night
By the light, by the light
By the silvery light of the Halloween moon!

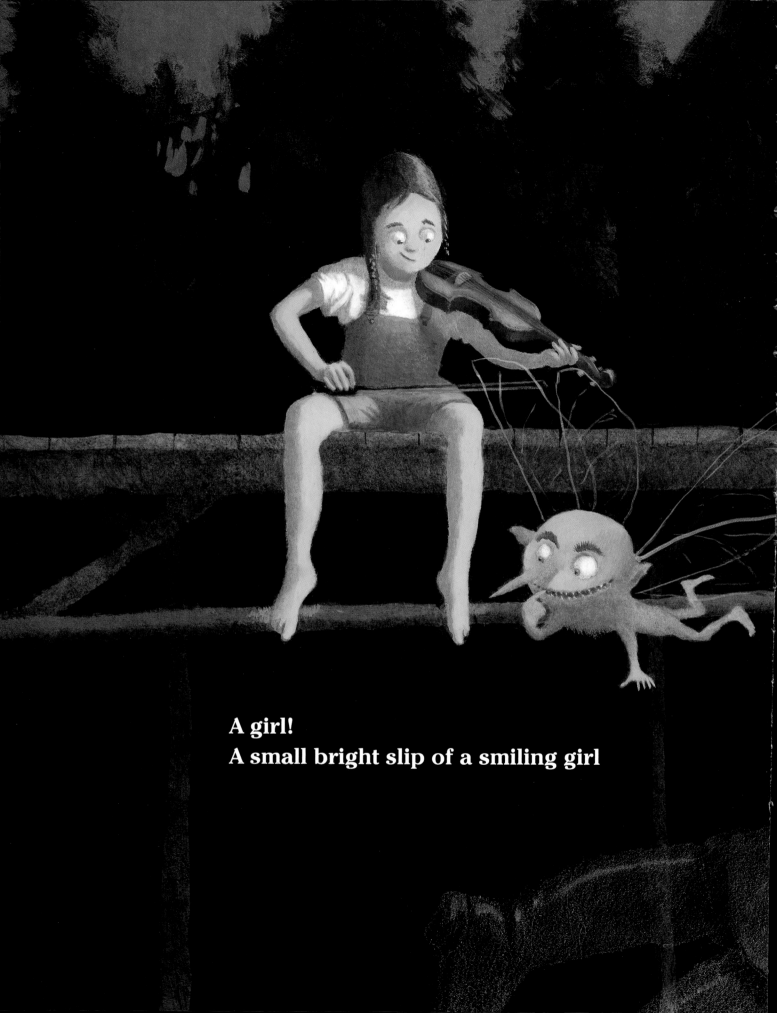

A girl!
A small bright slip of a smiling girl

Who smacks the sprite
Who bites the ghost
Who trips the ghoul
Who swats at the bat
Who bumps the witch as she snatches the cat
When he springs through the air to catch the toe
That taps a tune in the dead of night

By the light, by the light,
By the silvery light of the Halloween moon!